When a Smile Begins to Hurt

By Shaniqua Early

Edited by Krystal Berry
Cover Work by Aalia Tabassum

ISBN: 978-0-578-79824-0

After years of running and hiding
I am not afraid of the dark.
And though it comes too often,
I've learned to sit and be idle.
I've learned to embrace the shadows of what was
And find comfort in the whispers of what's to come.

And though life does not come with a rule book,
I put my game face on–
Protecting my every move,
Because they can't beat you if you've beaten yourself.
They can't tarnish what they don't know.
They can't hurt you if you wear hurt as an armor.

But eventually the armor comes off
And behind it is a broken little girl whose silence is loud.
Behind it is a misguided boy whose self-worth is reflected through self-hate.
Behind it is a nation with "a crooked smile that braces couldn't even straighten,"
Yet we smile anyway.
All of us–
Even when we don't want to or even have the energy to,
We smile.

So this book is for every person who smiles until it hurts.

ACKNOWLEDGEMENTS

I would like to thank my mother, Christel, and my father, Andrew, for always being supportive of my endeavors and goals that I strive to accomplish. Through your guidance, I am continuously developing into the woman I want to be.

I would also love to thank my brother and sister, Kellen and Sydney McNeill, for being my muse. I hope that you grow up knowing you can do anything you want to do and that I will ALWAYS be in your corner.

To my closest goal-friends, thank you for staying on top of me and holding me accountable. This book has always been an idea, and through your constant encouragement, it is now a reality.

Ebony Matkins, thank you for always being a mentor and unconditional friend. You have provided great feedback and support throughout this process.

Finally, thank you to all of my students–both past and present. Due to your stories and vulnerability, my characters are able to have a voice.

TABLE OF CONTENTS

CHAPTER 1

Staying the Course

"But with everything she had in jeopardy, she knew turning around wasn't a real option."

"Watch where you're going, jackass!"

These were the words from a man, yelled at Kendall, as he practically knocked her over with the wind of his bike. Startled, she instantly regretted coming here and wondered if this was a sign. She tried to find every excuse to stay in her dorm room, yet she found herself walking closer and closer to the dreadful unknown.

As soon as her alarm clock went off this morning, she spent the first ten minutes trying to gather her nerves. She knew that today would be uncomfortable, but nothing could be worse than the nine missed calls she had on her phone from Chris. With the biggest eye roll and in complete disgust, she slid out of bed to get dressed. Her roommate had company last night, so Kendall quietly tiptoed to her closet, walking past two half-naked people. *At least someone had a good time last night,* Kendall thought to herself. She stayed up late last night watching *Girlfriends* instead of doing some much-

needed studying, but must have been sound asleep when all the *fun* happened.
Luckily, she was a deep sleeper.

She definitely felt like it was a sweats type of day, but she was always told to make a good first impression. She reached in her closet to grab her favorite yellow blazer, but it had a pizza sauce stain, and Kendall hadn't found time to do her laundry. She looked at her laundry basket, in the corner of her room, overflowing with two weeks' worth of clothes. She instantly tried to go with the excuse that she had nothing to wear, but just as she was about to climb back in bed, she saw the stack of graded papers on her desk: *all F's.*
She had been trying hard to stay focused in school to maintain her scholarship, but she was dealing with too much at one time. Kendall stood up with a deep sigh. She reached for her cardigan that was bald up under two weeks' worth of homework, brushed her teeth and headed out the door.

Realizing that she was in the middle of the busy sidewalk, she quickly snapped back to reality and briskly knelt down to gather her things with every intention of going back home. But with everything she had in jeopardy, she knew turning around wasn't a real option.

People had always viewed Kendall as Miss Perfect. Because she was very good at burying her hurt, she appeared to have it all together. Kendall spent her time in high school doing everything right – to the point that she hardly exposed the things that were truly wrong. This created a division between her and her peers, because in the rare moments she did mess up, everyone treated her as if she did not have permission to. Therefore, she did not give *herself* permission to be flawed. She spent the past year in school hiding the fact that she was hanging on by a thread, and with Chris' latest stunt, the thread was two seconds from snapping. She looked down at the coffee stained note once more:

"Dr. Chanel Simmons' Office
1675 Park Lane
Suite 328
2nd Floor
First door on your left"

She slowly looked up at the building in front of her. After bobbing and weaving through rush hour traffic and many years of hesitation, she had finally made it. Her new and improved life awaited her behind the words of those directions given to her by her professor at school. As she stood in front of the building, she thought of all the baggage that she would be carrying inside with her. But with a deep breath, she put on her smile, placed the note in the pocket of her plain blue cardigan and opened the door to what would change her life forever.

CHAPTER 2

When a Smile Hurts

"I heard this is where you come when your smile begins to hurt."

"Dr. Simmons?"

"Ah. You must be Kendall," she replied.

"Yes. I am sorry that I am a little…" she found herself stuttering "…*late*."

Kendall immediately felt that she made a bad decision finding her way to this office. Here's yet another person to judge her – imposing on all of her insecurities. She took a deep breath and started again.

"I apologize for being late. I haven't quite gotten the hang of traffic on the new highway they've built."
The doctor smiled a very warming smile and replied, "You're never late when trying to be the best version of yourself. I know it can be challenging to try new things, and talking to a stranger can seem overwhelming. But you're here, and I'm so glad that you are. If you're not already, you will be too. Please, have a seat."

With the comfort of the doctor's inspirational words, Kendall sat down to begin her first therapy session.

She was rather tall, Dr. Simmons, or so she seemed. She was sitting in a fluorescent, pink upholstered chair – a beautiful accent to her black and white wonderfully decorated office. It had a lot more personality than what Kendall had seen on television shows.

In the seemingly long 15 seconds in between conversations, Kendall admired Dr. Simmons. She had great posture as she sat with confidence and her legs crossed. Noticing how neatly Dr. Simmons' clothes hugged her slim body, Kendall subconsciously sat up straight and intertwined her own legs to mimic Dr. Simmons'. This was a rather uncomfortable position, but a seemingly more appropriate one.

"Kendall, I see here that you are a junior journalism student at the local university. I am an alumna myself. How do you like it?"
Kendall wanted to instantly admit that school was extremely stressful, and she hadn't quite figured things out – even after three years of being there. Between working split shifts at the local coffee shop and having to travel to campus to be in class on time, Kendall never had the time to build genuine connections with people or establish strong friendships. She did, however, spend time with her now ex-boyfriend whenever he wasn't studying. The moments she did have to herself, she sat in her room listening to conscious rap or neo soul music. Music was a way for her to connect to words that she wished she had the

courage to say. She had a thing for lyricists and found comfort in the words of J Cole and India Arie along with others.

Still, Kendall was a writer at heart. She spent many nights writing poetry that she would never have the courage to share. There were many nights when she would pretend to be asleep as she listened to her roommate boast about how great college life was, with her friends, as they pre-gamed for parties or simply gathered in the room for girl time. Although they had extended the invite to Kendall in the past, Kendall declined. Having friends meant sharing and exposing her true self to other people, and honestly, Kendall didn't know who that was.

Recently, she had been longing for a social life that mirrored her facade as a journalist. She was the writer for the "Dear K-Knows" column for the campus paper–a very good one at that. People would write to the newspaper about all of the exciting and sometimes crazy things they were going through. And because no one knew who was responding to their concerns, Kendall was able to live vicariously through the words of others' experiences and her own advice. And since she and her boyfriend recently broke up, Kendall needed her distant interactions now more than ever. So instead of class, she turned to strangers to cope with her unfulfillment...until it backfired.

Kendall finally replied,
"It's great! I never knew that college could be both educational and eventful at the same time," the two of them laughed, "but I'm managing."

Kendall had always wanted to go to an HBCU. She had done plenty of college visits in high school, but the pride and self-awareness people possessed at historically black colleges and universities was what inspired Kendall. One time, her school took her to visit North Carolina A&T University. She'd heard so much about it, but nothing she heard compared to actually being on campus! The group she was with was sitting in the cafeteria eating when a young lady stood up in front of everyone and yelled, "I'm dangerously in love!"

Her yell *silenced* the entire room. Kendall, confused, looked around to find the root of the commotion and noticed that no one moved. Instead, everyone smiled at the girl and gave her their full attention. So, she continued:

"I'm dangerously in love
And the dangerous part about it is
I'm in it alone
Holding on to every image of the past
Anticipating the images to auto focus on our future
But they're blurred
Fading into what was.
You see we had the perfect storybook

But I guess every fairy tale turns tall tale
And your fairy dust stopped working a long time ago
Happily ever after wasn't so happy
And as unhappy as I was
I was willing to play princess
And await my prince's homecoming
But he never came."

The cafeteria went crazy clapping and yelling things like "Word!" and "Go off poet!" Kendall was mesmerized at the girl's courage to speak up in front of everyone and the energy of the room. She had never seen something so invigorating and that was how she saw her college experience happening. Going to college, even in her hometown, was supposed to be her moment to shed everything in her past and spread her wings into the future she wanted to have.
But not everything goes according to plan.

It was as if Dr. Simmons could see right through her. "I see here that you work at Tisley's Coffee Shop. I've heard great things about it. I'm thinking about trying it one day. How do you like it?"

Kendall didn't hate her job. It put money in her pockets so that she could get by and pay for books. She was on a partial scholarship, but that did not include all the trivial things college required of its students. Not to mention, she had to pay a hefty amount of money just to keep her car on campus so that she could get to and from work. She was one of the hardest workers at the shop. She always received great customer reviews and was very in tune with the locals and their orders. She was always smiling– despite what she felt on the inside.

"The coffee is really good. We have these homemade lemon pastries that are to die for. It's the customers' favorite. You should try us out!" Kendall replied.

"I think I will," she nodded.
Dr. Simmons had not dropped her smile since Kendall walked into her office. But her posture began to weaken as she leaned forward and crossed her dainty hands as if she were ready to move past the fluff of the basics. Dr. Simmons then asked, "Why do you think your professor felt the need to refer you to my office?"

"I don't know why," Kendall replied with a sudden irritation.

She flashbacked to why she and her boyfriend broke up. He complained that she was always too distant and wasn't vocal about how she really felt about the things going on in their relationship. Chris told her that she was emotionally *unavailable.*

Unavailable? No.

Drained? Absolutely.

Chris was always very needy. He constantly held Kendall accountable for his emotions and she could barely handle her own. Every time she turned around Chris was trying to mold her into the perfect girlfriend who he would marry someday. He expected them to spend holidays together with each other's family. He even wanted them to spend a certain amount of days together throughout the week. To most girls, that would be cute. That would be ideal.

However, Kendall did not want to be married. Hell, she did not know what she wanted. They were both extremely young, and she had never seen a successful marriage. Therefore, in her mind, marriage meant *control.* She spent her entire childhood being control by the people who were supposed to love and protect her, and she refused to give another person that much power over her.

The thought of her and Chris' future scared Kendall, but instead of telling Chris that his unrealistic expectations of her were adding unnecessary pressure, Kendall kept it to herself and continued to masked her true feelings. After all, she did love him. She just did not have the experience nor the energy to reciprocate. She knew that she was passive and nonchalant about a lot of things, but she couldn't admit that out loud– even if that meant pretending she didn't care when his sidepiece made her debut and ended their relationship.

She sent Kendall a letter about her and Chris' long and passionate night together. In the girl's defense, she had no idea who would read her letter or who she was even writing to, but Kendall knew it was for her. She had received an anonymous submission from someone on campus that said:

Dear K-Knows,
I know you know all about turning guys down– especially those with girlfriends. You always give the best advice and I'm hoping you have some for me. There's this guy in my chemistry class and I just know he's my soulmate. He gets my sense of humor and I definitely get his. He is super smart and has the highest GPA in our program. He pulled me aside after class one day and finally asked me for my number. I was super geeked because I wasn't going to ask him for his. I ain't that desperate (even though I really was). But anyway, great beginning to the perfect love story, right?

WRONG. He has a girlfriend.

She's this plain-Jane type of girl who doesn't even appreciate him. All he does is whine about how she's not attentive to his needs. So, I was. He came over one night to study…I promise. But one thing led to another and… let's just say, my feelings are in way too deep now. He hasn't broken up with his girlfriend though, so what should I do?

-Hopelessly In Love

Kendall felt her heart sink as she read the entry. Chris had been at the top of his chemistry program since being at the school. Her heart sunk even lower when she remembered she couldn't get in contact with him the other night, which was unusual for him. Chris was normally by the book, so she was furious that he would betray her like that. As if that wasn't bad enough, the plain-Jane comment really got her. She knew she was simple, but is that what Chris *really* thought about her? *Did he prefer a girl who was dumb enough to include distinct details that would get them both caught up?*

This wasn't Kendall's first experience with a thirsty girl ruining a relationship, and it probably wouldn't be the last. So, instead of responding rashly and publishing the letter, Kendall kindly taped the submission to Chris' dorm door with a note that read "Here's to our future!"

"Kendall? I see you're in deep thought. What is that?" Dr. Simmons asked.

"What is what?" Kendall responded.

"What is it that you're thinking about?

Kendall became very short, "It's nothing" she replied. She thought about sharing her break up and history with men, but she held back.

"Okay, you said you didn't know why your professor gave you my information. Well then why are you here? What encouraged you to come anyway?"
Kendall sat back in her chair, uncrossed her legs from their uncomfortable position, and folded her arms. As strong as she had been her entire life, a part of her was *tired.* So she finally let it out:

"I heard this is where you come when your smile begins to *hurt.*"

CHAPTER 3

Why Am I Here?

"I, personally, don't need help."

"They said I need help."

"*They*?"

"Yes. *They*. After nine months of marriage counseling, my wife and our therapist had the genius idea that the only way my marriage will work is if I get the individual help *they* say I need."

"Well it's not about what other people say. How do you feel?," Dr. Simmons, replied.

"I don't need help. It was my idea to go to marriage counseling."

Dr. Simmons sat up straight and said, "Well, Austin– are there some things that we may discuss, here, that may require individual attention? You know–without the presence of your wife?"

"What do you mean?"

"A lot of times, we are very open and honest with our loved ones about our past and upbringing. However, it's normal for us to create a wall that keeps others from unlocking doors we have decided to bolt shut. The constant struggle to deflect can cause displaced emotions. Emotions we are not aware of and, therefore, can't explain in marriage counseling."

"Again, I, *personally*, don't need help. I'm just doing this to save my marriage."

Austin relaxed his disposition.

"My goal in life is to help other people. Now, I've done a lot of things that I'm not proud of over the years. I grew up in an abusive household. I lost my best friend to gun violence in middle school. Shoot, I even lived in my car for weeks at a time at one point. But I'm here now. I am a happily married man, *on most days*, with two beautiful children that I would give my last to, but luckily, I don't have to. We live on the nicer side of town in a home we own. My kids play soccer and have found a love for music through their weekly piano lessons. My mother would've never been able to afford piano lessons when I was growing up. I'm making sure they have the opportunities I never had."

Austin was very happy with how he and his wife were raising the girls. It gave him a sense of redemption for things that he had done that he was not proud of.

Austin sat up straight and fixed his tie. He took great pride in his appearance and it showed in his soft green, wrinkle free suit. He placed his nicely manicured hands on his well-maintained beard and continued,
"I've experienced things, but I'm blessed. As much as I'm sure everyone, including yourself, Dr. Simmons, has the best intentions, sitting on a couch with a therapist, who wants me to revisit memories that were erased years ago, is a disaster waiting to happen– especially because as shocking as it may sound, *I AM YOU!* I am Dr. Simmons to 147 young minds eager to escape the rooms I have escaped. And to be strong for them, I am strong for myself. My strength benefits everyone– including my family. So, with all due respect, *doctor*, my life is constantly being played out for others to see daily. There is nothing that can be accomplished without my wife present."

Proud of his monologue, Austin sat upright in his chair with confidence that he had put Dr. Simmons in her place. He huffed, and with a smirk, he added, "I mean, it wasn't until I met my wife that I even found my purpose and desire to teach. She has truly made me a better man, and for that, I can look past any problems we encounter in our marriage."

After jotting down a few notes, Dr. Simmons smiled her usual smile and replied, "you're absolutely right! I praise you for breathing life into our youth. They need strong male figures to not only teach them, but to guide them as well. A lot of children don't have that male presence."

"Exactly!" Austin interrupted. "I know I didn't have anybody to look up to growing up. My grandmother did the best she could to raise me and my brothers, but she was a woman. It takes a man to teach a boy manhood. But honestly, being a man and being in the father and husband role can be overwhelming at times. And my wife doesn't understand that. She gets mad at me when I want to take a moment to unwind and be by myself. I take care of the house first though. I make sure the girls have done their homework, and I try to prepare dinner a few nights out of the week so that we can eat as a family–something I never had, and most kids will never know. I feel like I deserve a moment to myself occasionally."

"You definitely deserve some *you* time" Dr. Simmons noted.

"But my wife be trippin."

"Well, where do you go when you want to be alone?" Dr. Simmons responded.

"I drive wherever my car takes me and I park it. I sit. I relax. I reflect. And I come home."

"What does your wife say she dislikes about the time you take time to decompress?"

"She thinks I come back too late and more aggressive than when I left."

"Well, do you?"

"Yeah. It's normally pretty late."

"Do you come back more aggressive?"

"I mean sometimes I come home irritated," Austin hesitated. "But it's only because she likes to fuss about what I can and can't do. I'm a grown man!"
"Ahh." Dr. Simmons suddenly understood. "What type of advice do you give your high school boys who think they're grown and don't need school or your class?"

"You know, my students are at the age where they think they know it all. It can be aggravating because they can't see beyond right now. They are not aware of the real challenges of the world and how unprepared most of them are. I'm not going to lie, I was hard-headed at that age, so I get their lack of enthusiasm or connection to life outside of high school. That's why it is my job to help them find their purpose and be their guidance."

Guidance…

…a word Austin was far too familiar with. As a fraternity member, he was always taught that guidance was given to those who had the potential to guide others–whether good or bad. To be guided meant that you entrusted someone so much, that you allowed them to become a part of you. You allow them to influence some of your actions, thoughts, and decisions. You look to that person for insight. Guidance was the beginning of Austin's late-night car rides.

"Purpose." Dr. Simmons said.

"Huh? What did you say?" Austin quickly fled from his deep thoughts and became present in the office once more.

"You said you help your students find their purpose. You also said your wife helped you find yours. Maybe there's more to your strength as a man that you haven't identified yet. Maybe something is holding you back."
"Nah. I'm pretty much an open book," Austin interjected.

"I'm sure you are, but a lot of times, we give other people credit for doing things in our lives that we had the potential to do on our own. Sometimes we depend on other people so much, we believe we aren't capable of having the things we deserve on our own."

Dr. Simmons looked at her watch. She exhaled gracefully and reached to shake Austin's hand. "Great job today, Austin. I'll see you in two weeks."

Austin extended his hand in complete awe that Dr. Simmons would end their session with a very *heavy* and *judging* statement.

CHAPTER 4

It Is What It Is

"It is what it is though."

"You worked so hard, Brenton! What would make you go back?"

Dr. Simmons didn't even give him a chance to respond before going on with, "say it with me, Brenton. *Probation.* I am on probation."

"I know I am on probation, Doc, but no one is 'tryna hire me outside of the shop, and working on cars ain't paying the bills right now."

After two years of being clean from selling drugs, Brenton had been doing everything he could to stay focused and not revert to his old mindset. He stumbled across the auto shop one day, and saw the "Now Hiring" sign in the window. He didn't have much experience with working on cars, but the owner, Mr. Eugene, saw him looking through the window. Just as Brenton was about to walk away, the old man came outside and asked, "you look'n for trouble or work?" From that moment on, he had been working the front desk for the shop and did minor repairs. It wasn't his

ideal job, but in the beginning, Brenton was just happy to have legal work that put some money in his pocket and kept his probation officer off his back.
This was his second year seeing Dr. Simmons, and she had been very persistent in making sure Brenton did what needed to be done to change his old ways of handling things and to keep him out of jail. But old habits, apparently, die hard.

"How would Mr. Eugene feel knowing he took a chance on you and you're back to your unconventional ways?" Dr. Simmons asked.

Mr. Eugene was well known in the community for trying to reach the "troubled" youth. He hired Brenton knowing he had a criminal record.

"Mr. Eugene doesn't care that much. I'm just one of his charity cases and he reminds me every chance he gets. Don't get me wrong, I appreciate everything he has done for me, but I ain't lookin' for nobody's pity. Especially from someone who is only paying minimum wage."

"Well, you're also in the process of finding your mother. How would you feel telling her that you have a record, yet you're still risking everything by selling drugs?"

"To be honest Doc… I don't care. This is who I am."

"No, Brenton. This is who you continue to *choose* to be."

Brenton put his head down just enough for the doctor to still see his eyes. He'd always had a blank look on his face. Emotionless is how he had been described his whole life. But Dr. Simmons could always see past the emptiness he shared. She was very in tune with Brenton and his habit of putting up a wall when people got too close. And although he hated to open up about anything personal, he always felt very comfortable with the doctor.

"And stop saying you don't care. That's a defense mechanism. You *do* care. That's why you are in search of your mother. Being a drug dealer is not who you want to be. You want to be better. You want to *feel* loved."

Brenton did not respond. It was almost as if he wanted to agree, but he refused to. *He couldn't.* He didn't know what love was. Love, to Brenton, was the emotion he felt making drops and providing a fix for those in need. Love was *making that paper.*

"They say your mother is the first woman you love," Brenton began to speak again. "I knew that was a lie. Keisha was. No. Wait, LaTonya was… oh, no, Amaria was. Yeah. Amaria was."

It was nothing to him to be with different women knowing how invested they were in him. Brenton was very charming and could make any woman feel like she was his only, but in reality, Brenton couldn't attach himself to any of them. Women were easily disposable to him, and he would rather be by himself than to fully commit to anyone else.

"You see, my mother was my first heartbreak, and ever since, I've found comfort in the streets. I've found love in the game, and the game loves me back. And I know they say she's toxic, which is why when she started calling, after I got out of jail, I wouldn't answer. But like all toxic things, she was tempting, so I had to pick up eventually."
"The game?" Dr. Simmons knew exactly what Brenton meant by "the game", but she often had him explain things in detail so that he could hear and process his thoughts.

"Ever since the age of seven, I knew my hustle would be different from the hustle my case worker kept preaching about to me. She would tell me to go to school, because it was my ticket out of my unfortunate situation. Little did she know, I never looked at being in group homes and struggling as an unfortunate situation. It was just *my* life. I was dealt this shitty hand, and I had to learn how to play it. So, I went to school, but not because I liked it. It just allowed me to make the rules for my life instead of following the ones my social worker wanted me to follow. In school, numbers became my escape. I became friends with supply and demand and chemistry made me my own boss. I had to learn to make things shake–that was until I got expelled. Who knew using your knowledge attained at school could get you in so much trouble?"

Brenton shrugged his shoulders and, without looking at Dr. Simmons, continued. "It is what it is though."

CHAPTER 5

Fight or Flight?

"It's okay to want reassurance from other people sometimes."

"**W**elcome back, Kendall. I'm glad you decided to continue our sessions. How are you?"

Besides the fact that she was currently failing two out of four college classes and had been late to work every day this week, she replied, "I've been great. Never better."

Kendall's ex had been reaching out, more frequently, wanting to talk, but she left the "IMY" and "Baby, I'm sorry" messages on read. Over the years, Kendall developed a flight approach when handling situations. Instead of sticking around and putting up fight to deal with her problems, she ran away from them and never looked back. So, once she made up her mind that she was done with a person, she was completely done. The thing about running though, is if you're not careful, someone can easily come in and *trip you up.*

After some small talk and updating the doctor on her past relationships, Kendall inhaled and dropped some new information on Dr. Simmons.

"Now, there's this guy. He comes into the shop every day."

Kendall stopped as if she had just said something she wasn't supposed to. She always felt guilty for finding interest in a new guy so soon after ending things with another. She knew what it looked like to other people, and she never liked the judgement she thought people had. However, it never stopped her before, and it certainly didn't stop her now.
Kendall continued, "He orders the same thing: a large coffee with two creams, four sugars, and a slice of banana nut bread. He orders this each and every day."

"He must be very unforgettable if you remember his order."

"That's the thing. I never really paid attention to him until earlier this week."

"Oh? What was so different?"

"On Tuesday, he smiled at me and told me I had a beautiful smile."

"That must've made you feel good."

"Yeah, it did. I know it's only been two weeks since Chris and I broke up, but it has been even longer since I received a simple compliment. Chris always wanted me to open up and tell him how I felt about him, but he rarely acknowledged the things I did share with him or noticed something as simple as how I looked that day."

Dr. Simmons could see Kendall's self-esteem diminishing as she spoke about her ex. It was clear that this break up did more damage than Kendall realized. "It's okay to want reassurance from other people sometimes," Dr. Simmons began. "But we have to do things for ourselves. We have to be confident in our decisions because we may not always get that reassurance."

Kendall nodded in understanding. Deep down she knew that the guy's compliment filled a void that she had, within herself, in that moment. She was also aware that comparing Chris to a random person from the coffee shop was stupid, but for the first time since the breakup, at least she wasn't comparing herself to Miss "*Hopelessly In Love.*" She was a pretty girl with long, natural curls. She had *smooth*, dark skin that complimented her tiny waist and big ass.

It was annoying. Kendall thought it was bad enough the girl could mentally satisfy Chris, but when she spotted the two of them with a group of people, in the student union, she instantly understood what he saw in her. *Why would he want plain Kendall when he can have "big booty"– whatever her name is?*

"Tell me more about this mysterious guy," Dr. Simmons requested with interest.

"There's no more to tell. I haven't seen him since that day."

"He hasn't been in for his daily coffee?"

"No. It's like he knew he was never coming back. It was weird."

Kendall sat in deep thought. It bothered her that this nameless man left her feeling curious and unsatisfied. It bothered her that he was just a customer–nothing more and nothing less…until now. And after ignoring her ex's phone calls, it was nice to have something, or someone, to take her mind off of things.

CHAPTER 6

Caged Bird

"But in that moment, her wit told me her whole story."

"The last time I was here, you hinted toward the idea that I depend on my wife too much. That couldn't be further from the truth. And I don't know who you think you are insinuating that!"

Austin came in *hot*. He had been thinking about Dr. Simmons' last remarks ever since she dismissed him two weeks ago. He didn't depend on her, but he couldn't help but think that his wife saw something in him that he couldn't see in himself. He was dressed in disappointment and defeat when the two of them met six years ago. They met at a bar during Karaoke night. He was there by nature, but she was there by choice. She grabbed the mic to make her karaoke debut and in a matter of moments, she transformed.
As she sang and danced to "Drunk in Love" by Beyonce', Austin couldn't help but to instantly fall in love with the free spirit of the mystifying woman in front of him. After three drinks, he still didn't have the confidence to approach her. He kept asking himself, *"What would someone like her want with someone like me?"*

"I didn't mean to offend you," Dr. Simmons apologized. "I just know that no matter how much people help us, we have to make the decision to be helped. We are the catalyst of any change that we make."
Austin sat back in deep thought. He didn't make the decision to speak to his wife that night at the bar. She made the first move by buying him a Hennessey and Coke. She sparked the initial conversation, and he was eternally thankful that she did. He was a UPS truck driver when they met and was very complacent with his life. He always wanted more, but never had the drive to put his college degree to use. It was his wife who found the program that led him into the classroom. And yes, he had to choose to follow through with the program, but it took a lot of convincing on his wife's part.

"I commend you for making the decision to teach. I also commend you for finding purpose in what you do. And you're the only one who can find your purpose!"

"Thank you, Dr. Simmons." Austin felt encouraged. Although he was grateful for his wife's assistance, deep down, he was tired of her saying, "I got you this job," and "If it wasn't for me…" He secretly admitted that it was nice to hear something different for a change.

"So, Austin. Tell me about your daily routine" Dr. Simmons switched gears.

"What do you mean?"

"What are things you do on a consistent basis every day?" She clarified.

"How is this going to help me and my marriage?"

"Well if we look at things you do on a consistent basis, maybe we can identify some things that may unknowingly add pressure on you during the day. It can help us identify ways you can relieve stress throughout the day. And then perhaps you won't feel the need to decompress as often when you get home."

Every morning that Austin got ready for work, he got dressed, kissed his kids and wife, and left *almost* prepared to change lives. The last thing he did was make his daily stop at the local coffee shop around the corner from his house. A man needed his coffee, and there was something about a latte, extra whipped cream with a raisin bagel. He also enjoyed being able to catch up with the cashier who used to be his student a few years back. She was a straight-A student and was always involved in whatever event the school was hosting.

He remembered talking to her about all the great things she would accomplish, even growing up in a single-mother household. He knew her family struggled financially, but he loved that she wore a smile daily. She always smiled and worked hard– just as she did every morning when he walked into the coffee shop.

"After I leave the coffee shop," Austin concluded, "I pull up at work, put my game face on, and tend to the people who need me most."

"Most?" Dr. Simmons questioned.

"Yeah. That's what I said."
"You don't think your wife needs you… or your daughters?"

"Don't go twisting my words. I didn't say that. I'm just saying that a lot of my students don't have someone they can look to or talk to. My daughters do. I make myself available for them every day."

"I understand. I wasn't trying to change your words. I was only asking for clarity" Dr. Simmons apologized.

Austin didn't respond.

"Do your students ever frustrate you? Can they be difficult to manage sometimes?"

"Not at all. We have built a family environment, and though we all know how to push each other's buttons, we also know how to love on each other. I love my job. I love my students. They make me feel needed."

Austin seemed to take everything she said offensively, so Dr. Simmons thought carefully before speaking. "Do they make you feel needed in a way that your family cannot?" Dr. Simmons asked on edge of Austin's response.
"I guess. They don't tell me how to be the teacher. They allow me to lead and they willingly follow. It's not a constant power struggle like when I'm at home with my wife. Even my daughters test my parenting at times. It's nice to be the teacher most students confide in."

Austin began telling Dr. Simmons about a class discussion he had about five years ago after reading Maya Angelou's *Caged Bird.* The class talked about how the bird was a representation of freedom that the speaker felt she didn't have. But he then followed up the discussion with the question, *"Who could've taken away the speaker's freedom?"* His students gave a lot of different answers, but there was one response that stood out most to him.

Curious, Dr. Simmons asked, "So when she said that in front of everyone, how did the class respond?"
"They didn't. What she said was so encrypted that the other students were completely oblivious. She was always so witty. But in that moment, her wit told me her whole story."

"Did you say anything to her after class?"

Austin felt uncomfortable and Dr. Simmons could tell. He began to fidget with his fingers for a few moments before saying,

"On her way out the classroom, I gave her a silent nod. She gave a very faint smile and returned the nod." Austin sat back in his chair.

"I knew she felt comfortable with me and she trusted me with information that she had not told anyone. And that's why I love what I do. I create a safe place for my students."

Dr. Simmons leaned forward, pressed her lips together, and sighed lightly.

"It sounds like your students create a safe space for you as well."
After the session, Austin made his way to his car. Before pulling out of the parking lot, he just sat there, reflecting on Dr. Simmons' statement, and once again, thinking about his student from the coffee shop. He had forgotten about that particular class discussion and what she revealed during class. An intelligent young lady with the world at her hands–violated but still able to smile. In that moment, a cold spirit came over him. Haunted by his past, Austin reached into his glove compartment, reaching past the hidden steel tool and grabbed his fifth mini bottle of the day.

CHAPTER 7

Altered Smiles

"I have a way of altering smiles."

"**S**o, how was your day?" Dr. Simmons began.

As usual, nothing was unusual about his day. Brenton woke up inside of his small, one-bedroom apartment and sat at the edge of his bed. Thinking about his last session with Dr. Simmons and the pressure he's putting on himself to find his mother, he got dressed for work, grabbed his stash out from the drawer, and headed to the corner of Anderson Street to Tisley's Coffee Shop. He enjoyed his morning commute, because he was able to people watch as he walked to work. Since being released from jail, Brenton hadn't saved up enough money to buy a car. Luckily, the repair shop was only a few blocks from where he stays.

"Every day, I wake up, get my coffee and go to work. Nothing special or unpredictable ever happens to me."

Brenton could think back to a time where he had to constantly look over his shoulder because he never knew who was watching him. Time was money and money was time, so he was constantly making quick moves and living on an adrenaline high. This led to his downfall and resulted in him going to jail. This time around, he had been doing things differently. He was no longer addicted to the fast life. He found solace in working at the auto shop and bringing in his customers that way. This new norm was less suspicious and far more unpredictable.

"Really?" Dr. Simmons replied.

"The only thing that changes about my mornings is the cashier at the coffee shop I go to. I mean– she is always there, but her smile is different every day."

Dr. Simmons was surprised. This was the first time Brenton had mentioned this young lady and he seemed to brighten up as he spoke of her.

"Her smile?"

"Yeah," Brenton suddenly became very serious. "I've learned that people smile for one of two reasons: they are genuinely enjoying life, or they are trying to hide from life behind their smile.

"Interesting," Dr. Simmons noted.

"So, I never know if I'm going to get a genuine smile or a sad one. Either way, they're both beautiful.

"This young lady must be pretty special seeing as how we have spent most of our session today talking about her." Dr. Simmons gave Brenton a wink.

"Doc, I'm telling you," Brenton paused to gather his thoughts, "she's a natural beauty."

"Why don't you say something to her?"
"I did, today, for the first time. I told her that her smile was beautiful."

"What did she say?"

"Nothing. I didn't wait around for a response. I complimented her and left."

Dr. Simmons examined Brenton's body language. There he sat with his eyes gazing out the window. She could tell he wasn't really looking at anything and was in deep thought.

"Brenton?"

"Yeah, what's up?"
"Why didn't you engage in conversation? You seem to really be into her."

He let out a big sigh and replied, "I have a way of altering smiles."

CHAPTER 8

In Denial

"Alcoholic."

Alcoholic.

This is the word Austin's wife continuously tried to force down his throat, and he was tired of it. He wasn't an alcoholic. He didn't have to have a drink. He just wanted to. And though he ended his evenings with a drink or two, it was the morning drinking that also had his wife concerned. But it wasn't a big deal to Austin, because he mixed it with his coffee and never went to work drunk.

"If you don't need to drink, and you don't feel it when you mix it in your coffee, why do you drink it?"

Dr. Simmons posed such a simple question, but his response was far more complex. Austin's mother was his superhero. She would constantly take the beatings from his father, pick herself up, and walk out into the world with her head held high. She was a generous woman and was extremely selfless when it came to taking care of others. She was selfless to the point that she took every hit so that her son didn't have to. Though Austin resented his mother for staying, he admired her courage and strength, even if it came from the bottle. She would always smile at Austin and tell him that he didn't have to worry about anything, because "mommy has it under control" as she sipped her "superhero juice."

As Austin grew older, he understood that her drinking was a problem. But sometimes, masking the hurt feels a little bit better than dealing with it. And because his mother was so important to him, he learned to look past the damaging issues in their relationship as well.

"I don't think it's a problem. I'm not hurting anyone."
"Does your wife seem to think so?"

"She's just upset that she can't control everything. She thinks that the kids are intuitive and somehow knows whenever I drink. She feels like because she couldn't control her father's drinking, she has to control mine. I am nothing like her father!"

Dr. Simmons began writing notes. She normally did more listening than writing, but today was different.

"So, both you and your wife have a history with a parent who was an alcoholic?"

"My mom wasn't an alcoholic!" Austin snapped.

"I'm sorry," Dr. Simmons apologized–something she found herself doing constantly throughout their sessions. "You both have experience with parents who liked to drink around their children?"

She could tell that she still wasn't asking the correct questions to make Austin relaxed enough to continue with the conversation, so she changed topics in the hopes of trying a different approach.

"I was thinking about your student from the coffee shop you were telling me about last session. Why do you think she was comfortable sharing her story in your presence?"

"I don't want to talk about her today."

"But you seemed so enthusiastic about your experience with her. You were pleased thinking about the impact you had on her."

"I said I don't want to talk about her! In fact, I don't want to talk anymore today."

Austin stood up and brushed the wrinkles out of his clothes. He cleared his throat as he fixed his tie.

"I'm sorry, Dr. Simmons. I'll see you next visit."

With the doctor bringing up things from his past, in the first 15 minutes, she pushed a little *too* hard. Austin was able to maintain his cool in public, mostly. But he panicked when he felt like the doctor was trying to connect his drinking to his past. It triggered his inner demons once more, and he could tell that this time, a drink wasn't going to make them go away.

CHAPTER 9

Something Different

"I just know I care enough to leave it alone. Leave her alone."

"Doc, I'm not good with women. I always end up hurting them by leaving. And I know it's wrong, but I can't help it."

"So it's the chase you like?"

"I guess. She can be the baddest thang walking, but once I bag her, I don't want her. And then they start acting crazy."

"You don't think they have a reason to?"

Brenton rolled his eyes. "I ain't out here telling them I want to be with them or nothin'. It's not my fault if they out here falling for men they barely even know."

Brenton couldn't help but think about Tasha. He had explained to Dr. Simmons that the girl was obviously insane. They had spent a few nights together, but that was all. Brenton only called her over late at night and made sure she didn't stay too late into the morning. In his mind, she knew "what it was" between

them. But it was clear she thought something more of their time together. When he stopped calling, she started doing drive-bys and unannounced pop-ups. It took his little vacation to jail to stop her craziness. He still worries what she would do if they ran into each other again.
"Why do you think you lose interest in women so fast?"

"I don't know. You're the doctor. You tell me."
Brenton looked as if he really expected Dr. Simmons to know the answer to the question.

"That's a question only you can answer, Brenton."

"But you always ask me questions just so I can tell you more about me and my past. Then you say all these fancy things and yadda, yadda, yadda– just to tell me I'm the problem. But I know I'm the problem in this situation. I need you to tell me why."

"Brenton, my goal is never to make you feel like you are the problem. My goal is to have you reflect so that you can get to the root of your issues on your own."

"Yeah, yeah. I know." Brenton shrugged his shoulders with another slight eye roll.

"But I can tell you my observation." Dr. Simmons scanned through her notes looking for information from their past meetings. "You said a while ago that you feel like your mother abandoned you. You also said that she was supposed to protect and love you but was apparently too selfish to do so."

Brenton began to think about the many years he spent in foster care– wondering when his mother would come rescue him. He always had to look over his shoulder and be on alert, because he was smaller than the boys in his foster homes. After nights of fighting, discomfort, and mistreatment, he made up in his mind that his mother hated him. He vowed to never allow anyone to hurt him again.

"Yeah. She obviously loved herself far more than me because she left me. And ain't another woman gonna have that kind of power over me."

"It sounds like you prefer to leave the women so that they won't have a chance to leave you. I think it would trigger that feeling of abandonment you mentioned previously."

"I guess."

Deep down, Brenton knew Dr. Simmons was correct. He knew that he had never truly been interested in women outside of the desire to have sex with him. But the coffee shop cashier was different. He hadn't stopped thinking about her since he decided to go to a new cafe'.

"A new coffee spot? But why? We've talked about breaking routine. You only break it when something is wrong or you're about to make a poor decision."

Dr. Simmons was confused. The last time Brenton stepped away from his normal, he started selling drugs again. It worried Dr. Simmons, because she had developed a genuine concern for Brenton's well-being and his actions. Suddenly, Brenton's story about the coffee shop cashier started to sound very familiar, and that caught Dr. Simmons off guard.

"I broke routine to keep from making a bad decision this time. It's something about her that I can't turn away from. If I kept seeing her, I would've had to spit my game to her, and next thing I know, she would've been crawling out of my bed as I promised her that I'll call her later. But I won't. So I'm avoiding that. She looks like she knows hurt all too well."

He had watched her. Not on some creep stuff, but he happened to see her close up the coffee shop one evening as he was walking home. He overheard the phone conversation she was having with someone about not being able to maintain her scholarship because she felt overwhelmed. He found himself smiling because he never knew she was in college, on scholarship at that. She had brains and beauty. But as he continued to listen, she said that she could never ask *him* for help. And though Brenton didn't know *him*, he

knew that this person had caused her so much hurt and pain in the past. He could hear it in her voice.
"So I don't even want to do her like that. She has enough going on."

"And the other women you meet don't?

"I don't know, Doc. I just know I care enough to leave it alone. Leave *her* alone."

CHAPTER 10

He Took Everything

"He already took everything from me."

"She just makes me so damn frustrated!"

Kendall was becoming more comfortable in her sessions with Dr. Simmons. She found herself putting aside her facade more and more, and expressing her true feelings. Although she found comfort in her mother on most days, she couldn't talk *about* her mother *to* her mother. And she definitely couldn't talk about *him* to her.

"Do you think she understands your point of view? It sounds like there is a disconnect between the two of you."

Dr. Simmons had been seeing Kendall for a few months now, so her relationship with her mother had been discussed often. Her mother tried her best at providing for her, and though they struggled, Kendall knew how much her mother loved her. She knew she would give up everything to make sure Kendall finished school and worked toward accomplishing her dreams. The problem is her mother had nothing left to give.

"Clearly she doesn't understand. She told me she was tired of being the only one that had to sacrifice while my sperm donor lived comfortably with his family across town."

"I didn't know your father was so close. You never talk about him."

"Because I don't have a father."

"Has there ever been a time when he was actively a part of your life? "

"Oh, he was active alright…up until I was 6. My mother got a note from his mistress describing their affair in detail. She even described the inside of our home and apparently exposed all of the memories she had with me."

Kendall remembered hearing her mother screaming at her father. It was one thing for him to be unfaithful, it was a completely different story for him to bring his mistress around her daughter.

"So you knew about his infidelity?"

"I was 6. I didn't know anything about infidelity. I just knew that if he kept his hands on her, he would leave his hands off of me."

Dr. Simmons became still for a few minutes. She knew the silence would become uncomfortable for Kendall, but she wanted her to just sit in the moment. She had casually admitted to something and nothing all at the same time. She immediately connected the dots between Kendall and another patient of hers. Dr. Simmons was always very professional and knew that she couldn't say anything that would create a conflict of interest.

But she couldn't resist.

"Have you ever told anyone?"

"Told anyone what?" A look of regret cast a shadow on her face. She suddenly realized that she had reopened wounds that she had been trying to heal.

"You said your father wouldn't keep his hands off you. What do you mean?"

Knowing that she was already in too deep, Kendall decided to rip the band-aid off. "Let's just say my father had a fascination with little girls, especially his own daughter."

"Does your mother know?"

"No. My mother adored my father. She was so weak when it came to his charm."

Kendall remembered that later on in the evening, after her mother approached her father about his mistress and her note, she had watched her mother prepare his dinner plate and place a soft kiss on his forehead as she gave him his food. Typical.

"He would cheat, and she would look away."

Kendall fell into thought. She knew that deep down her mother knew what her father was doing. She stayed up many nights waiting for him to come home. She watched her mother scrub makeup out of his clothes. Her mother never wore makeup. She would hear her mother fussing with different women telling them not to call our house anymore. Her mother knew, but she pretended she didn't. She just smiled and catered to him until the smile became a little too heavy to hold.

"My mother doesn't understand why I would never ask him for anything. He already took *everything* from me. I was 6. I was young, but I knew it was wrong."

"So you've kept this to yourself all this time?" Though she was genuinely concerned, Dr. Simmons was looking for the connection between her patients.

"In high school, we read this poem by Maya Angelou. It was so beautiful, because it explained the misery a bird felt being trapped inside a cage longing to be free.

All of my basic classmates couldn't see past the birds. In their minds, she was clearly talking about birds and people needed to free them from cages so that they could roam freely." Kendall rolled her eyes in dissatisfaction. "So, I simply told the class that the poem was a metaphor for someone who is trapped by their experiences. I even told them that the poet was raped which is probably why she feels trapped in the first place. Of course my immature classmates laughed and brushed it off, so I told them that it wouldn't be funny if it had happened to them."

"So you told your classmates?"

"No. I wasn't really talking about me, and they didn't seem to think I was. But Mr. Howard, my English teacher, gave me a nod at the end of class. I felt like he heard me. Like really heard me."
"How did that make you feel?"

"Uncomfortable at first. He was a man. And so was *him*. But I knew Mr. Howard just cared, so I didn't mind."

"Maybe he was proud that you understood the poem on a deeper level."

"Maybe I should have been in Advanced Placement classes."

The two of them giggled. Dr. Simmons remembered Austin saying how smart and witty Kendall was. She also remembered the sadness she saw in his eyes when she brought Kendall up in their last session. Knowing what she knew now about his student, she knew she had to push Austin *even harder*.

CHAPTER 11

On the Defense

"Women always want to seem like the victim."

"She left me. I came home and all her stuff was gone. She took my kids, Dr. Simmons! My damn kids!"

Austin paced around the room in complete anger. Allowing him to vent, Dr. Simmons sat quietly, observing his every move and listening to every word. She noticed how antsy he was as soon as he walked into her office. He didn't have on his normal tailored suit and his shoes looked like they had been dragged through the mud. She listened as he yelled about his wife not understanding him and being selfish by taking the kids from their father. He even yelled about her cheating on him last year which is why they went to counseling in the first place. This was new news to Dr. Simmons.

"So she can sleep around like a hoe and I'm supposed to accept blame?" One dagger after another shot from his mouth. "I hate her. I hate all women."

Austin was often very confident about his relationship. Even through the regular marital arguments, he was always sure of the love the two of them shared. They were always very affectionate, and their intimacy was great…until it wasn't. Last year, he realized that his wife wanted him to touch her less and less, and their chemistry seemed to shift. Being naive and blaming it on the stress of work, he continued on with things as normal.

He had decided to rekindle some of their love by preparing a romantic candle lit dinner for his wife. He'd hired a sitter and even left work early to make sure everything was ready and perfect for her. She was so surprised that they didn't even make it through dinner before the two of them headed to the bedroom. Things were going according to plan– until she called him another man's name in the midst of what Austin thought was pure passion. But it wasn't. It was purely pathetic–pathetic of Austin to think his wife could be faithful after everything they'd been through.

Holding back personal emotions and understanding his rage, Dr. Simmons offered Austin a seat. Out of breath and shaking, Austin sat down. He was a mess. After getting off work and coming home to an empty house, Austin called his wife. She told him that she wasn't happy and didn't feel like he was making the changes he needed to make for their marriage. He tried pleading with her, but her decision was final.

Austin pulled out his phone and slid it across the coffee table that separated the two them. Dr.

Simmons hesitantly looked down at the lit screen. Her eyes reverted to Austin whose hands were now jittery. She took his silence as permission to look at the opened message on the phone.

You were supposed to love and provide for our family, but it's clear you only love yourself and the bottle. If you spent just half the time you spend in the bar or taking your late-night trips at home, with your family, we wouldn't be in this messed up situation. I love you Austin, but love should not hurt. I hurt every time you leave the house because I do not know which Austin I'm going to get when you return. I hurt when my daughters, OUR daughters, ask me why their dad is always sick. I hurt because I shouldn't have to look outside of our marriage for consistency and a real connection. I am not proud of, nor am I making excuses for sleeping with other men, but I need to feel something real. THIS isn't real anymore. Our happy family isn't real anymore. This angry, empty shell of a person you have become is running the people closest to you away. The girls have already witnessed the breakdown in our marriage; I refuse to allow my kids to stand around and watch their father kill himself because he doesn't love them enough to put the bottle down.

Dr. Simmons gently placed the phone back on the table.

"Women always want to seem like the victim. Just because she feels guilty that she stepped outside of our marriage, she wants to flip the script and blame my drinking. I'm the empty shell? Only a heartless person will cheat on their husband and find a way to blame that shit on him! I've been in too many situations where women do something and then point fingers."

"What other situations?"

Austin hesitated. As he began to relive his past, he was more ashamed than anything. He knew that *she* was a victim, but it was easier to blame the young lady than it was to look at himself. He didn't even want to go to the party that night, but he desperately wanted to be a part of the fraternity. His dream was to be amongst a brotherhood that stood for excellence and he would've done anything to join.
And he did.
"Never mind."

"Austin, this is a safe space. Sometimes you have to talk about these uncomfortable things in order to heal–in order to move on."

"I can never move on. I'm just one big screw up, and honestly, I'm tired," Austin said with great defeat.

Austin walked out of the office. He knew he could never verbally admit he hurt that woman or his role in her trauma. He never laid a finger on her, yet he felt completely responsible for her rape. She was half naked in her neon yellow bodysuit. It was haltered and hugged every curve on her body. She tried to play hard to get, but it was clear she was into the homie...not the rest of the of them.

The homie walked over to her and whispered in her ear. She giggled. The two of them disappeared for a little while before he brought her upstairs. Austin knew that when she walked through the door and saw all of them instead of a private room, she regretted everything before that moment. But by then, it was too late.

Normally, a glass or two of Hennessy would wash away this agonizing memory. But this time, the pain lingered, so Austin didn't stop drinking until the pain was gone…or the bottle– whichever went first.

CHAPTER 12

Don't Screw Up

"Don't screw up."

"I went back to the coffee shop this morning. After our last session, you really had ya boy thinking. I'm always 'gonna do girls dirty if I go in with the intentions to. And I don't wanna do that with her. Kendall is her name."

"Oh, wow. So you talked to her this time. I'm impressed."

Dr. Simmons was genuinely happy for Brenton. She knew how hard it was for him to look beyond his past experiences that gave him his guarded mindset. She was excited that he wanted to do something different this time.

"No. I didn't talk to her. But I did look at her name tag. One step at a time, Doc."

The two gave a silent agreement and revisited the topic of his mother. It had been three months now since Brenton decided to look for his mother. This task only became important when Dr. Simmons encouraged him to face some of the issues from his childhood to better understand why he continued to make poor decisions. They both decided that understanding why his mother abandoned him would provide answers to the questions he didn't know he had.

Brenton, with the help of Dr. Simmons, reached out to his old case worker to seek information about his birth mother. The relationship between him and his case worker was extremely rocky. She couldn't see past his hard exterior and made it clear that she couldn't wait until the day he was old enough to leave the system. On his 18th birthday, she gave him a card and said, "Don't screw up." That's all he had ever done, so he took it as a "fuck you" and threw the card in the box with all the memories he wanted to forget.

After months of trying to track her down on Facebook, he found her. She was now "Addison Walker" instead of "Addison Brown." She had gotten married and started a family of her own. After stalking her profile, he realized that she didn't really dislike him, she was unhappy with herself. But she had now found her joy. She found her happiness in her new life and it was time he found happiness in his. So he messaged her.

"Has she responded? I know the anticipation has been a pain."

"She has. She said she was no longer a case worker because she decided to focus on herself. She actually apologized for how careless she was with me.

"That must have made you feel good."
"It is what it is now. She did tell me that everything I needed to know was in my 18th birthday card she gave me." Brenton looked frustrated. "I don't know where that shit is! I wanted no parts of her or that jacked up foster care system."

"That's understandable, Brenton. Have you tried looking?"
"No."

Brenton was very short with Dr. Simmons. He knew that if he found the box with the card, he would have to really come to terms with whatever was behind the words… and he wasn't quite ready.

CHAPTER 13

Dear Mama

"Dear Mama"

"We talked for hours! Before I knew it, it was 3:30 in the morning and I still didn't want to get off the phone. I had to be at work by 6, but I was willing to deal with the consequence of not getting enough sleep. One minute we were debating on whether or not J Cole is underrated, which he *clearly* is, and the next minute we were talking about life and our childhood. I have never felt this comfortable with someone so soon."

"He sounds pretty charming."

Now aware of the entire situation, Dr. Simmons remained as neutral as she knew how.

"Charming? He's amazing!"

Kendall couldn't stop smiling. Brenton was so attentive and found different ways to make her feel special. She had told him about her problems in school, and although he had never gone, he knew exactly what to say to give her a positive outlook on her purpose in school. This was different from Chris who she never felt comfortable opening up to. He would always dismiss Kendall's feelings. Kendall felt appreciated again. She no longer wanted to give Chris and his apologies anymore of her energy because she refused to be like her mother.

But she was just like her mother–always finding the next guy to distract her from the last. Kendall vowed to take time for herself and focus on getting her grades up, and then Brenton pops up: tall, slim, and chocolate…just how she liked them.

She decided to take a different approach with Brenton than she had done with Chris. She decided to lay it all out on the table. She explained to Brenton about where she felt things went wrong in her past relationship. She knew she didn't voice a lot of things in the past. It was too early to get too serious with Brenton, but if they were going to be in each other's lives, even as just friends, she wanted to do things differently. So she chose to be vulnerable and told Brenton about *him*.

"You have a lot going on; do you think you will be able to maintain your scholarship while building a relationship with this charming gentleman?"

"I got this. I always do."

Kendall had spent her whole life balancing. Being emotionally happy encouraged her to do better, and to be better. There was something about Brenton that inspired her to work harder. He was special, but they had barely scratched the surface of what was going on between them…and for some strange reason, she trusted Brenton.

He told her about growing up in foster care and how it gave him his tough exterior. He had gone from house to house which forced him to fight constantly. He was always the "new boy" or the smallest, so he did everything he needed to do to survive. A lot of times, it was the adults he had to be on guard with the most. He had told her about one lady in particular that he stayed with. She forced the boys to find ways to bring in money for the house. She would always tell them that living with her was a privilege and that they had to earn their beds. Most nights, she would send them out to hustle. Brenton said he became good at it, and he had been hustlin' ever since.

Some women would frown upon how he makes his money, but it didn't bother Kendall. She was more intrigued by his intelligence and experiences. Everyone has a story, but the ending was up to that person. She could tell that Brenton was working to write an alternative ending to his story but needed someone to support him. And honestly, *she needed the support as well.*

"Just be careful." Dr. Simmons said in a worried tone. She knew what Brenton was capable of. Although she had faith in his growth, selling drugs was the one lady he wasn't willing to release. And when a man tries to juggle a double life, he's liable to hurt someone–even himself.

Dr. Simmons switched the subject, "Did you do your homework?" She had challenged Kendall to write a letter to her mother telling her all the things she wished she could say in person. Kendall found it extremely difficult. She was swamped with schoolwork; *how could she have time to pretend and write a pointless letter?*
"Yes." But I don't know if it's good."
"It's not supposed to be "good;" it's supposed to be *true*" Dr Simmons said, reassuring Kendall.

She grabbed the balled-up paper from her bag and read her letter aloud to Dr. Simmons.

"Mom,
You know I love you…. Blah blah blah."

Dr. Simmons quickly interrupted. "The purpose of this exercise is for you to emotionally invest in your healing, Kendall. Deep down, you're still the same little six-year old who needed her mother at a time where she felt most vulnerable. *Be that vulnerable little girl.* Take this seriously."

Kendall rolled her eyes, took a deep breath, and started again.

"Mom,
You know I love you. From the moment I was able to understand the feeling of love, I knew that was something the two of us shared that no one could ever take away. And no one has. However, someone has taken away our transparency. There was a time where I wanted to share every part of who I was with you, but I felt like you were always too busy sharing every part of you with other people.

Men.

Men are the other people, mom. You gave them everything you could, while you gave me the leftover pieces. I know you did everything, we had everything we needed and that I didn't have to go without, but in hindsight, I went without an emotionally present mother. The thing I needed to tell you most, I couldn't. I didn't want to disturb the peace in our household, and I didn't want to take away your happiness. But I know now that you weren't really happy, mommy. We lived in that house for years, both of us, going through the motions and allowing him to control us. I watched him take advantage of you every day, and you let him.

What kind of woman is that? What kind of woman allows her husband to take thirty minutes to tuck her daughter in at night, most nights, without seeing for herself what the "tuck in" process looked like. Since you never cared to know, let me tell you. "Tuck in" was the worst part of my days. I would hide and cry– not because I didn't want to go to bed, but because I didn't know what version of him was putting me to bed.

Some nights, he would actually come in and read stories to me, but there were many nights where my father touched me, mommy. He violated me on a consistent basis, and that is something I had to deal with on my own. That's why I could never ask him to do anything for me. He's done enough!
That was only the beginning of me losing you. I've been fighting for your love ever since you felt like you failed at your marriage and started looking to other men to make you happy. Apparently, I couldn't do it."

Kendall had a tear in her eye, but she quickly wiped it away before it could fall. "This isn't real. She will never see this" she kept whispering to herself.

"That was good Kendall. How did that make you feel?" Dr. Simmons asked.

Kendall thought back to Tupac's song "Dear Mama." It was one of her favorite songs because he was able to express his authentic feelings about his childhood struggles without devaluing his mother and her struggles. It was lyrical genius-ness but most importantly, it was *raw*. But Kendall wasn't Tupac and didn't believe she had the right to say these things to her mother.

"It made me feel like I don't appreciate all the great things my mother has done for me. She doesn't deserve to read this letter. She's a warrior, but even warriors have flaws. I don't think it's fair to point them out."

Dr. Simmons nodded in agreeance but quickly contradicted her nod with, "But is it fair for you to be a caged bird?"

CHAPTER 14

The Weight of Guilt

"I didn't even help her."

"**R**eally, Austin?"

Dr. Simmons didn't normally show disappointment, but at this very moment, she couldn't help it. Austin had called her shortly after their therapy session last week discombobulated. Dr. Simmons could tell he was spiraling because of how he was dressed, but the phone call confirmed it. He kept saying that he was sorry, and he never meant to hurt *her*. Not really understanding, she pleaded with him to turn around and come back to the office, but he refused. She tried calling him back, and left messages every day since. She was surprised when he showed up on time for his appointment today.

"I was just exhausted. I had a very long day, and I'm still dealing with the fact that my wife left me! I couldn't focus, Dr. Simmons" said Austin, trying to convince both the doctor and himself.

"What about what you said on the phone to me–right before the accident?"

"I was tired. That's all. I'm fine. My car is fine. Now, that fence is another story, but my neighbor and I worked it out. I'm paying for the damages."

Austin tried to make light of the situation. He hadn't been to work in over a week and no one seemed to miss him. The school reached out to ensure he had a doctor's note when he returned, and his wife didn't even come by after she heard about the accident.

"You know, she didn't even come see me. *When did she start hating me to the point where she won't let me see my kids?*"

"Had you been drinking at the time of the accident?"

"I had one drink. That's all. I wasn't drunk or anything. Just tired." Austin hoped that the more he said it, he would believe it. But he didn't. He knew he had more than one drink. He had one in the parking lot before leaving Dr. Simmons' office. He had stopped at his favorite bar across from the neighborhood auto shop. As a regular, he had his usual: Henny and Coke.

"Are you sure?" Dr. Simmons didn't want to seem pushy, but she wasn't buying anything Austin was saying.

"Yes. I'm sure."

While Austin sat at the bar and had a couple drinks, he overheard a few people at the bar talking about some "Brent" guy from across the street. As he continued to eavesdrop, he overheard them saying how the kid had everything to make you feel good. Austin was not new to certain substances. He had experimented with a few things in college, but that was a thing of the past. Although they sounded tempting, Austin vowed to never put himself in the position to make the same mistakes as the ones he had made in his past–especially ones from *that* night.

After sitting at the bar for three hours, Henny didn't seem to make the pain go away. He left his wife five voicemails, and she wouldn't return his calls. Suddenly, the weight of the world became extremely heavy and he desperately wanted to lighten the load. He was so miserable that a trip across the street to the auto shop was becoming more appealing…so he obliged.

Big mistake.

"Austin, are you ready to be honest? I know it is hard facing reality, especially with everything you have going on, but I promise you will feel better when you release your true feelings. *Trust me.*"

Oddly, Austin immediately found comfort in her words. He knew that he couldn't take anymore sleepless nights, and he couldn't afford to crash into another fence. He took a deep breath and replied,

"Okay."

Once he began to open up, he couldn't stop. He had told her how he didn't feel like a man once his wife cheated. It started with one evening drink just to be able to look her in the face. One drink turned into two, and before he knew it, facing her became unbearable. He would leave at night to drink and came home upset because he couldn't stop thinking about her disloyalty. He explained that he had always thought he would be the one to ruin their marriage because of his past, but it was her who had forsaken, what he thought was, a happy union.

"And you know what her excuse was? She told me I cared more about them damn kids at school than I did her. She said I gave all my attention to everyone except her." Austin's eyes became sad. "I didn't mistreat her. I didn't disrespect her. I did not cheat on her. *I just wasn't good enough.*"

Dr. Simmons just sat and listened. For once she felt like Austin was beginning to acknowledge his hurt as opposed to covering it up. However, Dr. Simmons was not ready for what she heard next.

"We were so young and dumb! I just wanted to join!"

Tears began to form as Austin caught them with his shirt sleeve before they fell.

"It was my first college party, and I just wanted to have fun and get in good with the bruhs."

Suddenly feeling uncomfortable, Dr. Simmons began to squirm in her seat. She sat there and listened as he told her about how the president of the organization brought a fine girl up to the room where they were all chillin'. She was clearly drunk but was obviously feeling him. The two of them had been dancing all night and you could tell how both of them had plans on how they wanted the night to end. When she came in the room and saw nothing but guys, it was like she instantly became sober.
"I could see the fear in her eyes. She knew what was about to happen even before I did." Austin couldn't stop his tears any longer. "I didn't even help her. I watched them hold her down as I froze."

That was a defining moment for Austin. Four months later, the event was a thing of the past, and he was now a member of a strong brotherhood. He wore his letters with pride–even if he gained them at the expense of a girl's innocence.

Austin began beating his hand against his forehead, as if that would somehow erase the memory.

Dr. Simmons became choked up listening to Austin's story and had to excuse herself for a moment. When she returned, she cleared her throat and asked, "whatever happened to the girl?"

"I never saw her again. Not even on campus." Austin scrunched up his face. "I don't even remember what she looked like. I just remember the gut-wrenching fear I had that night, and it has haunted me every day since then."

CHAPTER 15

Cold Blooded

"I know this may be disappointing, but at this point, I believe I'm protecting everyone involved."

Dear Brenton,

I never thought I would see the day that I would hear from you. Your mother and I decided years ago that giving you up for adoption was best. 22 years ago, your mother was in a very difficult and unfortunate situation. She was completing her junior year in college and had plans to start her doctoral program directly after graduation. She was so ambitious, and we had her whole life planned out. Becoming pregnant with you was damaging to that plan and being a single mom wasn't in the plan at all. I tried to talk her into taking alternative measures, but she refused. She was extremely strong-minded. I knew to look at you would bring her pain, and I was only trying to protect my daughter.

She had gone through enough hurt and disappointment with the entire situation. I told her men were no good, but she didn't listen. She ran behind some boy and got knocked up and he never called her again. She couldn't even find that bastard on campus, so she dropped out. I talked her into giving you up to someone who could provide the things she couldn't– someone whose plan you could be a part of. She went to therapy for years to get over things, and eventually she moved on. She got her degrees and never looked back.

I would like you to find comfort in knowing that our decision was not an easy one, but necessary. I say all of that to tell you that your mother has moved on. She has always resented me for making her give you up, but I was doing what was best for her. She said I didn't help or protect her when she needed me most. Well, now is my time to help. Please do not reach out to me anymore after this, and do not try to find her. Your mother has healed and has accomplished all the things she set out to accomplish. I know this may be disappointing, but at this point, I believe I'm protecting everyone involved.

-Chanel Carol

"The bitch said she's protecting me? She doesn't even know me! She's protecting herself and that dumb-ass daughter of hers!"

Brenton paused for a second.

"And then she wants to rub in how well my supposed mother is doing since she decided to give me up? I'm out here struggling! Struggling to stay out of jail and struggling to love myself! I've found a great girl who wants to give me all of her love, and I can't even accept it! I don't even know what it feels like for a woman to genuinely love me, or better yet, reciprocate it!"

Brenton continued to ramble on as he looked at Dr. Simmons to reassure him or give him her normal professional spill. But she just sat there with a blank look– *speechless*. Brenton took that as a cue to continue.

"And that evil Addison Walker… I mean Brown, or whoever the hell she is now, set me up! I found that stupid birthday card she gave me. She tried to make it seem like she actually cared about me. But no. This was part of her plan. She 'gon say *Happy Birthday, Brenton. You're grown now, but if you're ever feeling like a lost little boy, reach out to Chanel Carol, I hear she's a great listener.*"

Brenton took Dr. Simmon's silence as permission to continue.

"So I went back to Facebook, and all I found was this old lady named Chanel Carol. I thought about everything we've talked about, Dr. Simmons, so I had to man up and reach out."

Dr. Simmons tried to get her thoughts together quick enough to assist Brenton during his breakdown, but she couldn't. She remained in her seat and watched him self-destruct.

"I told her my name, birthday, and the reason I was reaching out. I told her that it was probably far-fetched contacting her– seeing as how I didn't understand who I was even contacting. I even told her that I got her name from my case worker and sent her a picture of the birthday card. I really wasn't expecting much from the old lady, but I definitely wasn't expecting this!"

After talking for 30 straight minutes, without the input of the doctor, Brenton plopped down in the chair across from Dr. Simmons.

"As if going through the terrors of the foster care system wasn't detrimental enough, Walker encourages me to reach out to this selfish woman? I'm glad I didn't look at that card until now."

All at once, Brenton realizes that Dr. Simmons hadn't interjected once. When she did finally get the nerve to say something, she said,"I'm so sorry, Brenton. I'm not feeling too well and really need to go home. We will need to reschedule."

Dr. Simmons gathered her things and hurried out of the office, leaving Brenton in the chair–*neither one of them knowing that this was their last session together.*

CHAPTER 16

Dear K-Knows

"Dear K-Knows"

Kendall never thought she needed therapy. She was so good at pretending that she even convinced herself that there was nothing she would gain from it. But the more she saw Dr. Simmons, the more she found it important to talk through the realities of her life instead of covering them up. Kendall's grades had been improving since seeing Dr. Simmons, and she stepped away from her "K-Knows" column at school after reading an entry that struck a nerve:

Dear K-Knows,

I spent my entire high school career working hard and being at the top of my class. I was involved in everything I could possibly be involved with and it made me really happy. However, I don't feel like high school prepared me for the disappointments of college. I am a freshman student and I find myself homesick and eager to go back to what I feel is comfortable. I have considered dropping out, not because the work is difficult, but because I feel like a nobody walking around campus. No one knows me or the great things I accomplished before getting here. I know I am strong, and I have the support of my friends and family, but I don't know how much longer I can smile through my conflicting thoughts.

-Sincerely,
The Unsatisfied Unknown

Kendall always had advice for the people that wrote to her even if she had never experienced it. But she found herself reading a letter that she could have very well written herself. The only thing is she was a junior, and by now she should have things figured out, but she didn't. So, she thought long and hard about her response. She thought about all of the tools Dr. Simmons had instilled in her. She thought about her own battle with finding her place in society– especially one that seemed to work so hard to ignore her.

She replied:

Dear The Unsatisfied Unknown,

Believe it or not, you are not lost and unimportant. You are in a stage of redefining who you are and how you want others to see you. Think of this as an opportunity to have a clean slate, and you have the power to create whatever picture you want without the expectations of others. It will be uncomfortable, but it will be necessary–just don't sit in confusion too long. Trust me, K-Knows :) You don't want to look up your senior year and feel like you never took advantage of everything college had to offer.

Love Always,
K-Knows

It was through that response that Kendall realized how she had been wasting time being concerned about the wrong things. She figured she couldn't help someone else before helping herself. She felt it was time that she stopped hiding behind the words of her advice column and lived in her truth.

There was so much she wanted to say now, but Dr. Simmons had been MIA for a while now. Kendall was no doctor, but she knew that breaking routine for some people can be destructive to all of their progress. If Kendall knew that, Dr. Simmons had to have known that.

Right before clocking out of work one evening, Kendall's boss told her that some lady came by looking to give her something. He said the lady ordered a lemon pastry and left a card in a pink envelope that she insisted he gave her. He remembered suddenly when Kendall explained that due to finals, she would not be back to work until the following week. He handed her the pink envelope with Kendall's name written in script. She had no idea who it could be from, but she opened it as soon as she made it to her '99 Honda Civic.

Kendall,
I spent years going to therapy to help me with my past, and I don't think it was by coincidence that you have come to me for that same guidance. From the moment you walked into my office, I knew you were someone who was going to have a difficult time

being honest with yourself. I was determined to help you look past the image you created and be able to come to terms with who you really are. But consequently, I've had to look at myself.

"I see so much of me in you. There was a point in my life when I had to make a decision: either I was going to allow my circumstances to define me or I was going to let them drive me. I chose the latter. College brought me my biggest hurdles, but I jumped over them and ran without looking back. And that's my biggest regret. I am writing to you to tell you that I, too, was violated and was too afraid to tell my mother. I spent my life allowing other people to control the decisions I made, and I gave men the power to strip me of my innocence."

Kendall could not believe her eyes and what she was reading. She knew she was not the first, nor would she be the last person to be touched or raped by someone, but she *never* would've thought this to be the case with Dr. Simmons. She was poised. She walked as if the weight of the world could never bear her down. Kendall had always admired how Dr. Simmons didn't just appear to be satisfied with her life, but she seemed genuinely grateful for her contribution to others and their mental growth.

After reading and re-reading the letter that was written so delicately yet emotionally, Kendall felt a sudden spark in her desire to become who she wanted to become. It wasn't fair what she had to deal with growing up. It wasn't fair that she shared the common secret of so many women who felt the need to stay silent to protect people who didn't even find it essential to protect the woman. And in the words of Dr. Simmons, *"It is our task to choose how we carry our burden, even if it disappoints others."*

The only thing she could think about was how Brenton needed her. The two of them found a safe space in one another where they felt free to unzip the disguise they wore daily. They needed each other...*or so Kendall thought.* Kendall knew that who she really needed was her mother.

It was unfortunate that Kendall would not be able to continue to see Dr. Simmons, but in that letter alone, Dr. Simmons challenged her to change the course of her life to ensure it reflected who Kendall wanted to be– in spite of everything she had been through. Even if that meant giving up her new "situationship." She was tired of seeking validation from outside people–especially from men. Though she knew Brenton authentically cared about her, he was broken, and two incomplete puzzles don't create a whole one.

She had been looking for a reason to change her major from Journalism, and this letter confirmed it. There was a new calling on her life, and it didn't involve investing large amounts of time and energy into a man or depending on another person for emotional support.

It also didn't involve being responsible for her mother's feelings. *She had her own to protect.* So she took the balled-up homework assignment from Dr. Simmons, ironed it out neatly as possible, and labeled it "To Mom."

With much reluctance, she had dinner with her mother and *handed her the note.*

CHAPTER 17

Fear and Frustration

"...our feelings always find ways to resurface when we least expect them to."

Austin stood confused in the middle of Dr. Simmons' office. Weeks had passed and Dr. Simmons had been unavailable for all of her appointments. This was unusual because she didn't take personal leave and would never leave her clients hanging. Though he had only been seeing her few months now, he was certain that her absence was suspicious. He also thought her timing was inconvenient seeing as how he needed assistance with controlling his emotions and decisions now more than ever.

Austin had been angry with the doctor because it was like Dr. Simmons opened the floodgate and left him drowning without the proper tools to survive. So, when he got the call that she wanted to resume sessions, he was hesitant. But there he stood, in an empty office with a pink envelope addressed to him.

Austin Howard.

Confused, he opened it:

Austin,
I learned a long time ago that you can't run from your past. You have to sit in it and deal with it before you can heal from it. The sit and deal with it aspect is what a lot of us have a hard time doing. We automatically resort to finding things to avoid how we feel and assume it is dealt with. The problem with that is that our feelings always find ways to resurface when we least expect them to. I, myself, have skipped over the necessary process when trying to recover from past pain. My time with you has only rekindled my suffering from long ago–suffering that you helped to create.

Austin could not believe what he was reading. How could he have created suffering for a woman he met only months ago. He thought back to a conversation they had had in the past when he accused all women of being victims. Here was another lady blaming Austin for something he clearly could not control. It wasn't his fault that Dr. Simmons had experienced hardships. It wasn't his fault that she chose to ignore the things she had gone through and pretended to be fine. Austin had spent his whole life feeling responsible for the misfortune of the woman from the party, and he was tired of being the scapegoat for everyone else.

Frustrated, he crumbled the letter up in mid-sentence and shot it in the trash can. He missed. He picked it up and shot it once more and missed again. This only made him even more upset. He left the paper on the ground and walked out of the office. He didn't care what Dr. Simmons had to say–at least that's how he tried to convince himself.

He stood outside the door of her office as he tried not to let the idea of not knowing get the best of him. He was familiar with the feeling of someone leaving him without a proper explanation, so why should this time be any different? Austin headed toward the elevator and waited. In the 15 seconds it took for the elevator to arrive, curiosity got the best of him. Before he knew it, he was in his car with the wrinkled paper in his hand once again.

*****

Austin couldn't believe what he had just read. There's no way that after 15 years, he coincidently ended up at *her* office out of all people. After driving aimlessly for almost an hour, Austin ended up in the parking lot of the bar. He was there so often nowadays that it almost seemed second nature to go there anytime he was not able to manage his thoughts. Just as he was reaching the door, he had a sudden urge for something a little stronger. After trying to process everything that was revealed to him in Dr. Simmons' letter, he decided to pay the auto shop a quick visit before entering the bar, however, when he got there, the doors were locked. There was no Brent in sight.

He found himself mumbling things–trying to understand how his past could be so daunting to show up in his present life. He knew it had caused a rift between him and his wife for some time now, and she didn't even know what happened. *But this was altogether different.*

Austin began to shake, feigning for something to take away the anxiety of what he had to now face. *He was feigning for something to make it all go away.* Austin got into his car to try to pull it together. His thoughts were becoming louder and louder, so he reached into his glove compartment for his emergency bottle, but it was empty.

He began to panic.

The bar was right in front of him, but he wasn't stable enough to be in front of other people. He felt himself spiraling, thinking about his last visit with Dr. Simmons. He had been so honest with her, yet it backfired like everything else in his life. Feeling defeated, Austin reached for what was available in the compartment: his tool.

He thought devoting his life to the success of the youth would somehow make up for his mistake of not coming to the rescue of that girl the night of the party. He was trying to be the best husband and father, despite the demons he struggled with. But it wasn't good enough. Nothing was ever good enough.

He wasn't good enough, and Dr. Simmons made that *very clear.*

CHAPTER 18

A Million Possibilities

"There were a million possibilities, but there was only one outcome."

"I always enjoy when you come in to visit, Chanel. It seems like it was just yesterday that you first came to see me. Now look at you– a beautiful and successful therapist yourself. That makes me happy because I consider you my little protege."

"And you know I appreciate everything you've done for me. You have been a great mentor. Who else can say their therapist is their friend?"

The two of them smiled at each other with gratitude. Chanel and Dr. Taylor had a very unique relationship. It had only been seven years since Chanel went from a patient to an intern in Dr. Taylor's office. She had nurtured Chanel while steering her in the right direction to open her own private practice. If it was one thing Dr. Taylor learned about Chanel, it was that even in her brokenness, she was strong. And it was that strength that united the two women.

"How is everything going? I haven't heard from you much since you opened your own office. Things must be going real well over at the Carol office!" Dr. Taylor was extremely proud of Chanel.

"Actually, I finally took my husband's last name, so now I go by Dr. Chanel Simmons. It took months of arguing, but I made the compromise."

"Oh, wow! Well, I know how strong-willed you are, so if you gave in, he must really be worth it." Dr. Taylor stood and gave her a warm and inviting hug.

"He is."

Chanel had been genuinely happy in her marriage and was glad she was finally able to embrace a man's touch.

"I also think it was time for me to rid myself of my mother's name. It was time for me to step out of the shadows of who she wanted to be and create an identity for myself. I'm not just her daughter anymore. I am a mother and a wife, and I finally feel like I have control over certain aspects of my life. My husband has been very patient with me."

"I love to hear that." Dr. Taylor's smile faded, and she dove right in. "Now, I know you almost better than you know yourself. You're not here to gloat about your thriving marriage, are you?"

Chanel knew she couldn't hide anything from Dr. Taylor. Dr. Taylor is the reason she is able to maximize growth with her own patients. They were both very good at reading people and sensing pain–even when hidden. So instead of trying to convince her otherwise, she gave Dr. Taylor *all the tea.*

"I know I can't tell you everything because of patient-client confidentiality, but does that apply when a patient's history includes you?"

Chanel knew how crazy it sounded as soon as it left her mouth, but Dr. Taylor had a way of deciphering Chanel's jumbled thoughts.

"What do you mean?"

Chanel started from the beginning. Dr. Taylor knew of her experience of being pregnant and having to deal with the painful experience of giving the baby up. She knew that Chanel wanted her baby, but had a standard to live up to–to please herself, but through therapy, she realized she wanted to please her mother. Her mother always encouraged her to be successful, but Chanel always found herself trying to live out her mother's dreams and not her own. Chanel never thought that the day would come where she could accept and move on from giving up her child for her career, but everyday made it a little easier.

"So, you still haven't discussed the entire situation with your mother?" Dr. Taylor asked without judgement.

Chanel continued to tell Dr. Taylor of how her mother was raped when she was younger which caused her not to see her value and worth. She would always tell Chanel to live the life she never deserved to have. Unintentionally, her mother created a barrier where Chanel couldn't discuss anything with her that didn't align with what her mother wanted her future to be.

That included that night at the party.

Dr. Taylor interrupted,

"You know that night wasn't your fault, Chanel. I don't want you going back down the path of blaming yourself. And as far as the baby, you all did what you thought was best for him. He had an opportunity to grow up and be loved by a family who could be all-in. It's okay if that family wasn't yours."

"But he didn't."

Chanel's eyes began to water. She was normally good at holding back any emotion that showed a sign of weakness, but in this moment, she felt vulnerable.

She continued to tell Dr. Taylor that the baby boy did not have a good life. She explained how important it is for anyone to have their mother because she is supposed to be a child's first love. She explained that she could live with the hope that maybe she did what was best, but she couldn't take the disappointment of being her child's first heartbreak.

"We've talked about this. There are a million possibilities and ways to spin your adoption story, but if you focus on the negative, you'll never be able to move on. I thought we agreed that whatever his circumstances were, they were better than knowing he was a product of rape."

Chanel was hysterical at this point. She laid with her head in Dr. Taylor's lap and in an instance, she became that scared and lonely college girl from all those years ago. Dr. Taylor proceeded to wipe Chanel's tears as she was baffled by the rest of the story.

"There were a million possibilities, but there was only one outcome."

Chanel told her about one of her patients and how he spent his whole life believing his mother was a coward. He turned to the streets for affirmation because the foster care system never gave it to him. No one tried to place him with a loving family, so he spent his life on street corners and trap houses until he rented his cell in jail. She explained that the sad part is, he was a good boy. He was lost, but not by his doing. His thinks his mother hated him and gave up on him before ever giving him a chance, and that is all he would ever know.

"He will never know that his mother could never hate anyone. He won't know that she really did give him up hoping that he would actually have a fair chance at life. He won't know that she prayed for his protection and safety every day. He could never know that his father was one of three rapists who held her down against her will. He will never know that his mother was broken into pieces and divided up between every man who stood in that room and did not come to her rescue."

At a loss for words, Dr. Taylor held Chanel tighter, and the two sat in silence.

CHAPTER 19

Open Scars

"I am referring you to another therapist."

It had been a week since Brenton last saw Kendall. After pouring his heart out to her and explaining his abandonment issues, he couldn't believe that she allowed someone to get into her head about him. He had been honest with her from the beginning. She knew he sold drugs, and she knew that he had a record. That didn't seem to bother her before. He was slowly beginning to invest so much into Kendall–both his time and emotions. But she reminded him why he never allowed anyone to get too close.

It was early last Monday, and Brenton was waiting for Kendall outside of the coffee shop. This had become a new daily routine for the both of them because Brenton thought it was important to start his day off with a beautiful smile to go with his coffee. *But this particular morning, Kendall wasn't smiling.*

Her eyes were puffy as if she had been crying, and when he tried to console her, she pushed him away. He had sense something was wrong when they spoke yesterday, but he had no idea that she wanted to stop seeing him. She mentioned something about hurting her mother and being in a process of a rebirth, but he honestly stopped listening after she said they had to stop seeing each other. The two of them sat on the patio seating before she went in for work. She explained that she had been seeing a therapist about her childhood and the impact it has had on the decision she made. Of course he understood because, he had been seeing a therapist for the *same* reasons.

"I realized that I've always looked to men to give me validation that only I can give myself. I know you are a good man, but you're not good for me at this point in my life. Honestly, there are things you need to figure out and work on before you can be a good man for anyone."

Those words were disappointing to hear–especially from Kendall. He had thought of numerous different ways that he could respond and try to persuade her that he was right for her, but he cared about her too much to lie. He believed that he could be a good man, but knew there was a lot of work to be done.

After getting that message from his "grandmother," he was in no position to be emotionally available for anyone else–mostly because he had chosen not to return to Dr. Simmons, because of the embarrassment he felt after she walked out on him.

He decided that silence was the best response. So he simply placed his hand softly against Kendall's face and gave her a slow, passionate kiss and walked away.

As he reached the door of the auto shop, he checked the mail like he did every morning before opening the garage. There was never anything for him, so he placed the mail on his boss' desk. Right before turning away, Brenton noticed a pink envelope with his name on it. Bewildered, Brenton took the envelope and went to the back of the shop. His first customer came in, and before he knew it, Brenton was flipping bags and cars until the shop closed.

As he was cleaning up for the evening, he remembered the letter he stashed in his bookbag. The last letter he received he didn't open for years, and when he finally did, he regretted it. But he decided that he couldn't always choose to run from things he was afraid of. So, with hesitation, he opened it.

My Sweet Brenton,

I know you haven't heard this a lot throughout your life, but you are special. Over the past two years, I have been able to get to know you on a level that no one else has. You have established great progress since we have been working together, and I only want to see you advance even more. However, I am referring you to another therapist. I know you will be reluctant, but I'm hoping that when you do decide to reach out to someone, you reach out to her. She has taught me all that I know.

His heart didn't want to continue on with the letter, but his mind had to understand why Dr. Simmons would let him go as a client. He thought they had a bond, the only bond that he truly cherished over the years.

There are a lot of things you do not know about me, but how could you? You were the client. My job was to listen and support you. But I am at a point in my life where I have to seek support from someone else, and as part of the process, I have to be honest with myself and everyone that I care about.

Brenton could sense that Dr. Simmons cared, but there was something liberating about her actually saying it.

As a young woman in college, I was taken advantage of. That experience was something I could not control, but the decisions I made afterward I could.

After finishing the letter, Brenton sat in the middle of the auto shop floor. Although foreign to him, he was pretty sure that he was crying–something he had *never* done.

Made in the USA
Columbia, SC
28 November 2020